Making New Friends

A special book written for you by

Dr. Gary

Illustrated by

Chris Sharp

All rights reserved. Published in the United States.

Library of Congress Control Number:

ISBN: 978-0-9904942-0-1

"Dragonflies aren't scary at all,"
thought the little girl, as she watched one
dart through the garden and flitter-flutter
around her.

"Are you trying to cheer me up?"
she asked sadly. But the dragonfly ignored
her and flew away.

The little girl sighed, "I miss Emily," and
continued wandering about her yard.

Feeling very lonely, she prayed for a new friend.

Suddenly, the little girl heard something strange and stopped walking.

"Ribbit, ribbit."

"What's that noise?" she whispered, listening very hard,

"Ribbit, ribbit."

When she looked down, she saw a small, green creature with icky-looking skin.

"Is that a frog?" she asked herself out loud.

"Indeed I am," the creature chuckled. "Don't be afraid."

"WOW! I didn't know frogs could talk,"
said the surprised little girl, "Do you
have a name?"

"My name is Larry, but my friends call me
Leaping Larry. I'm a good leaper.
I can jump very high and
very far."

"How high can you jump?
Can you jump into my lap?"
She asked.

"Of course I can," he said.

"Well, then show me,"
she said, leaning over to
get a closer look.

"Okay, but first can I ask you some questions?" asked Larry.

"Sure," said the curious little girl.

"What's your name?" Larry asked,

"Cindy. Cindy Susan McDoogle."

"That's a pretty name, Cindy."

"Thank you," she smiled.

"Do you have any brothers or sisters?" Larry asked.

"I have a younger brother and a baby sister. And guess what? Tomorrow is my birthday!"

Cindy replied.

"Really?" Larry asked.
"So is mine!"

"Tomorrow is your birthday,
same as me?" Cindy asked.
"Gee! Same-day birthdays."

"I have one more question,"
Larry said. "Why are you so sad?"

Cindy looked down at Larry.
A tiny tear slid down her cheek
and landed on Larry's head.

"I'm so sorry," she said. "I didn't mean to
cry on you."

"That's okay," Larry said. "It's only a drop
of water, and you know how frogs love water.
You don't have to tell me why you are sad
if you don't want to."

"I miss my best friend, Emily," Cindy said. "She used to live next door. Her dad got a job somewhere else, so they moved away."

"If my best friend moved away, I'd be sad too," Larry said.

Then, just as fast as you can say "ribbit, ribbit," Larry jumped high in the air, did a forward somersault, and landed in Cindy's lap.

"See?" Larry said. "I told you I could do it. Ribbit, ribbit."

Cindy laughed and laughed. "Ribbit, ribbit," she said. "I like you, Leaping Larry!"

"I like you too, Cindy Sue McDoogle," he said. "I like you too."

When Cindy and Larry finally stopped laughing, she looked down at the green creature. "Do you have any brothers or sisters?" she asked.

"I have 17 sisters and 10 brothers," said Larry.

"You do?" Cindy asked.

"I sure do," he said. "And you know what? All of us have a birthday tomorrow."

"Really?" Cindy said. "All of you were born on my birthday?"

"Really," Larry said. "Would you like to know how it happened?"

"Yes, please tell me."

"One day, my mom laid her eggs by the pond behind your house. A few weeks later, the eggs hatched and out came lots of tiny tadpoles, including me," Larry said.

"We swam around in your pond and grew bigger and bigger. Then we turned into frogs. So you see, all of us were born on the same day and have the same mom and dad."

"So you and your brothers and sisters are like a bunch of twins, or triplets, or however high it goes, right?" Cindy asked.

"Right," Larry said.

"I love your story!" Said Cindy.

"Say, I've got an idea!" Cindy shouted. "Why don't we have a birthday party tomorrow? We can invite all of your brothers and sisters and your parents and my family. We can have ice cream and cake and balloons and all the things frogs like."

"And we can have a leaping contest and sing," Larry said. "Frogs love to sing, you know."

So, Larry and Cindy arranged a fun-filled party in her back yard. They played games like hide and seek, had balloon rides for the frogs, sang goofy songs, told stories and laughed themselves silly.

Larry's family blew out candles, and ate ice cream and cake for the very first time. They all agreed it was fun to learn new things from new friends.

Both families gave the party two thumbs up!

Of course, Larry won the leaping contest.

Cindy was so happy, all she could say was "ribbit, ribbit" and burst out laughing.

Even though she still missed her friend Emily, Cindy was tickled pink that a frog like Larry could be so much fun.

Who would have guessed how quickly a little girl and a talking frog could become best friends?

Perhaps Cindy's prayer for a new friend had been answered after all!

The End

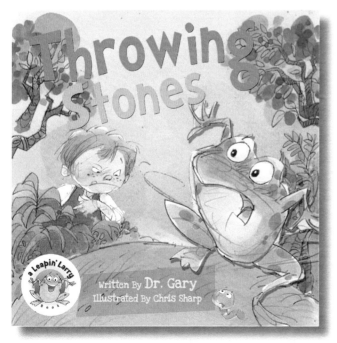

Do you like Leaping Larry and Cindy Sue McDoogle?

Then let the adventures continue! Look for these books, and discover what this lovable duo is up to.

- Show and Tell
- Leapin' Larry's Scary Adventure
- Throwing Stones

Dedicated to

six terrific grandchildren:

Emma, Lindsay, Sarah, Rebecca, Ali and Laura

&

all children who have lost a friend.

A special thanks to Steven Kulkis, who helped get this book started!